RUDOLPH THE RED-NOSED REINDEER®

Adapted by Rick Bunsen

Illustrated by Arkadia

A GOLDEN BOOK • NEW YORK

© 1998 The Rudolph Company, L.P. Rudolph the Red-Nosed Reindeer © & ® The Rudolph Co., L.P. All rights reserved.
Published in the United States by Golden Books, an imprint of Random House Children's Books, a division of Penguin
Random House LLC, 1745 Broadway, New York, NY, 10019, and in Canada by Random House of Canada,
a division of Penguin Random House Ltd., Toronto. Golden Books, A Golden Book, A Little Golden Book,
the G colophon, and the distinctive spine design are registered trademarks of Penguin Random House LLC.
All elements from the 1964 "Rudolph the Red-Nosed Reindeer" television special under license to Character Arts, LLC.
randomhousekids.com
ISBN 978-0-307-98829-4
Printed in the United States of America   45 44

Christmastown, also known as the North Pole, is the wonderful place where Santa Claus lives with Mrs. Claus, all the elves, and the flying reindeer that pull Santa's sleigh every Christmas Eve.

Nowadays, Christmastown is a happy place. The elves make toys. The reindeer fly. But in the old days everyone had to watch out for the Abominable Snow Monster. He was big and furry and hated anything having to do with Christmas. And he liked to eat reindeer!

All that started to change when Santa's lead reindeer, Donner, became a papa.

"We'll call him Rudolph," said Donner, looking at his new son. Suddenly Donner and Mrs. Donner saw a bright light.

"He's got a shiny red nose," said Donner in surprise. "I'd even say it glows."

Santa came to see the new arrival. But then he saw Rudolph's nose.

"Let's hope this glowing stops if Rudolph wants to make the sleigh team," Santa said. "We can't have any shiny noses flying through the sky!"

So the Donners put a little cover on Rudolph's nose.

Soon it was time for the new fawns to go to the reindeer games. There they would be inspected by Santa, who would choose the best reindeer for his team.

At first Rudolph felt shy. But soon he met a doe named Clarice.

"I think you're cute," she told Rudolph.

The coach arrived to teach the fawns what they needed to know to be on Santa's team. "First, we'll learn to fly," he told them. "You have to get up enough speed and jump into the wind."

Rudolph was so excited about his new friend that he took off with a great *whoosh!* He soared high over the heads of the reindeer, and Santa, too.

But as all the young reindeer continued to play, the cover popped off Rudolph's nose. It glowed for all to see.

At first the other deer were frightened. But soon they began to laugh and call poor Rudolph names. "Rudolph the red-nosed reindeer," they jeered.

And the coach said, "Go on home. From now on, you can't join in any reindeer games."

Only Clarice didn't laugh at Rudolph.

Poor Rudolph wandered off alone. Soon he met an elf
who was hiding in the woods.

"My name is Hermey," said the elf. "I want to be a
dentist, but right now I'm just an elf who doesn't belong."

"And I'm a red-nosed reindeer," sighed Rudolph.

The pair decided to be friends and to run away together. They hadn't wandered far when they heard the terrible roaring of the Abominable Snow Monster!

"It's my nose!" said Rudolph. "The monster sees it and is coming after us."

Rudolph and Hermey were saved by Yukon Cornelius, the greatest prospector in the North. "Jump onto my sled," said Cornelius, "and we'll run like crazy!"

But no matter how fast they went, the monster stayed close behind. Finally they were trapped at the water's edge. Cornelius chopped the ice with his ax, and the friends floated safely away.

They floated all night and landed on a strange island, where they were greeted by a puppet that sprang from a box.

"I'm the official sentry of the Island of Misfit Toys," said the puppet. "My name is Charley, and that's why I'm a misfit toy– no child wants to play with a *Charley*-in-the-box!"

"We want to travel with Santa Claus in his magic sleigh," said a misfit doll. "Otherwise, we'll miss all the fun with the boys and girls when Christmas day arrives."

The friends met an elephant with polka dots, a choo-choo train with square wheels, a water pistol that shot jelly, a bird that swam, a cowboy riding an ostrich, and a boat that couldn't float.

"We're misfits, too," said Rudolph. "Maybe we could stay here with you."

But the king of the island would let them stay for only one night. "This island is for toys alone," he said. "A living creature cannot hide here. But you can help us. When you return to Christmastown, tell Santa about these homeless toys. I'm sure he can find girls and boys who would be happy with them. A toy is never happy till it's loved by a child."

That night, while Hermey and Cornelius slept, Rudolph lay awake.

"My nose will only bring my friends more danger," he thought. "I must go off on my own."

But as he wandered alone in the snow, Rudolph realized that he couldn't run away from his troubles.

Rudolph returned to the mainland and headed for Christmastown. But first he had to pass the cave of the Abominable Snow Monster!

As he did, Rudolph heard voices crying, "Help! Help!" Rudolph rushed inside.

There were Rudolph's parents and Clarice! They had been searching for Rudolph and had been caught by the monster, who was about to devour Clarice!

"Put her down!" Rudolph cried, butting the surprised monster with his little antlers.

Just then, Hermey and Cornelius pulled up outside the cave. They had followed Rudolph's trail and knew he needed help.

"An Abominable Snow Monster will never pass up a pork dinner," said Cornelius. "Hermey, you sit outside the cave and oink like a pig. When the monster comes outside, watch out!"

OINK OINK

Hermey approached the mouth of the cave. *"Oink, oink,"* he
called. The monster dropped Clarice and rushed outside. At that
moment, Cornelius pushed a giant snowball down on top of
him—*splat!* Working quickly while the monster was stunned,
Hermey used his dentist's tools to remove the monster's teeth.

Back in Christmastown, Rudolph told how he and his friends had defeated the Abominable Snow Monster. Everyone realized that misfits have their place, too.

Rudolph told Santa about the misfit toys. "As soon as the storm lets up, I'll find homes for them," Santa promised.

Then the weather elf handed Santa his report. Santa gasped.
"The storm won't subside by tonight. I won't be able to see to
fly my sleigh!" Suddenly a flash of light caught Santa's eye.
"Rudolph," he said, "what a beautiful, wonderful nose! Won't
you guide my sleigh tonight?"

"I'd be honored to," said Rudolph, putting on his jingle bells.

"Okay, Rudolph," said Santa. "First stop is the Island of Misfit Toys. Up, up, and away!" And with Rudolph leading the way, Santa soon found loving homes for all those lonely toys.

"Rudolph the Red-Nosed Reindeer," everyone sang, "you'll go down in history!"

And he did!